The Da
Dile...ma

CW00381575

Anne Davies

CHAPTER ONE

"Are you okay Margot?" Lucy asked, once she was sure her father had left the room.

Margot took her hands away from her face and looked up at her younger sister and replied, "I'm fine Lucy don't worry. Has he gone?"

Lucy nodded and whispered, "I'm sorry I didn't help you."

"Don't be a nincompoop," said Margot smiling softly, "What would you 'ave been able to do, if you 'ad? No, you stay out of it. There's no point both of us getting a beating."

Margot had a cut across her eyebrow, where her father's knuckle had made contact and a bruised left cheek, but she was used to it, so stood up and grabbed a cloth, wetted it slightly from the nearby bowl and dabbed her face gently.

"How's Ma?" She asked.

"She's okay, I think 'e took most of 'is anger out on you." Lucy replied.

Margot was eighteen years old and the oldest of seven children. With dark brown curly ringlets falling across her shoulders, soft full lips and hazel eyes that always looked on her siblings with kindness, Margot was naturally beautiful.

To her family she was loving and generous and would do anything for them. Well, that is apart from her father, whom she hated with a passion. He was a bully and expected those around him to do everything to make his life easy. Late at night Margot would lie there, secretly wishing that he would die during the night, then feeling guilty for such wicked thoughts.

Lucy looked at her sister, whom she adored. She knew Margot took the brunt of their father's anger and she couldn't begin to tell her sister how grateful she was for that. Margot nodded thankfully at her younger sister.

"That's good, I'm stronger than our Ma."

A look of anger flashed across Lucy's face.

"You shouldn't have to be. None of us should!"

Margot smiled at her sister, who as she grew older became more and more like Margot, both in looks, but also in temperament.

Margot loved her mother dearly, but was disappointed in the way that she'd never been able to stand up for herself when father started beating on her. Margot thought back over her childhood and realised how much her mother had changed over that time.

When Margot had been a young girl, her mother had been much more bubbly. She'd played games with them to keep them out of her father's way, but as the family grew, it had become more difficult to keep the children quiet and so her father had become more angry and her mother had withdrawn into her own shell. As the eldest, it had been up to Margot to help out with her six younger siblings.

She didn't blame her mother, she had done her best, but years of abuse from her husband had made Mabel weak and downtrodden. Walter would regularly arrive home late, obviously the worse for wear, after stopping down the alehouse on the way home and he'd find fault in something that Mabel had done.

Margot knew that her mother did her best to protect

her children, especially the younger ones, pulling them towards her to protect them, but she was too frightened, and Walter seemed to enjoy upsetting her by making her watch as he took his anger out on the nearest child.

Walter had had a hard life growing up and his own father had beaten him, so for him it was normal to do the same to his children. He worked hard, but most of his money was spent in the pub with his work mates.

He would give Mabel a pitiful allowance and if she dared ask for extra to make sure they had food on the table, he would erupt into such a display of anger, that she'd learnt not to ask, but to scrimp and save instead to make sure they didn't starve, sometimes gong without food herself, to make sure the children were fed.

Luckily, for the others at any rate, Margot bore the brunt of their father's beatings. She could be quite headstrong at times, and sometimes couldn't help herself. She would answer back when Walter complained about the lack of substance to the stew or when the bread was stale. This would always earn her a beating. She didn't mind as long as it meant that her siblings were overlooked.

The small tenement home only had one bed, where Mabel and Walter slept with the youngest in between them. The rest of them curled up together, with a tattered blanket to keep them warm. It wasn't the best place to bring up a family, but Mabel always reminded her children that things could be worse.

"You could be in the workhouse, or homeless." She would say, if any of them moaned about the lack of space.

CHAPTER TWO

Margot's younger siblings ran wild, but her and her sister Lucy helped their mother tie wild flowers into bunches to sell around the streets of London. They enjoyed getting out of the cramped apartment, even though London was dirty and smelly, it gave them a chance to see how the other half lived.

"How come some of us are so poor, scrubbing about to find a penny, when these lot all seem to have more money than they know what to do with?" Lucy asked her sister, as they wandered up the cobbled streets of a nicer part of the city.

"I don't know." Replied Margot. "It's just the way it is."

"Do you think we'll ever be rich?" Asked Lucy.

Margot turned to her sister and laughed gently. "I doubt that very much." She replied. "No. We need to be satisfied with our lot and just get on with it."

Lucy nodded, "I suppose so, but say we did have some money. What would you buy?" She asked wistfully.

Margot laughed and thought for a moment before responding.

"I think I would like a huge cream cake, with jam and ...." Her voice trailed off, as she realised that she didn't really know what was in the cakes. She'd seen them in the window as she'd passed by, but had never been lucky enough to have spare change to go in.

Lucy looked at her with big eyes. "Oh Margot, wouldn't it be wonderful if we could afford a cake like that. I can feel my mouth watering, just at the thought of it."

"Me too." Said Margot grabbing Lucy's hand. "Enough of this dreaming. We got to sell these posies, so we got enough to buy some bread no matter about cake."

Lucy reluctantly let her sister lead her down the

street, towards two couples walking towards them.

"Wanna buy a posy for your sweetheart?" Asked Margot cheekily to one of the gentlemen.

The man looked down at her and smirked. "What have we got here?" He asked, turning towards his companions.

"My dear, would you like a tussie mussie? Help these poor children out?" He asked one of the ladies, pointing at the bunch of flowers that Margot and Lucy were offering towards the group.

She smiled sweetly at the posies. "They look very sweet. Yes, I'd very much like one. Why, thank you, Mr Brooks."

The man took one posy and looked at his friend. "Aren't you going to buy one for Miss Goddard?" He asked cheekily.

His friend smiled and nodded, turning to the young lady by his side he asked, "Would you like some flowers."

Miss Goddard blushed and lowered her head. "That would be lovely. Thank you."

Margot and Lucy couldn't believe their luck. They hadn't been out long and already had some coins in their pocket.

"Today's going to be a good day. I can feel it in my waters." Margot said, smiling at Lucy. And she'd been right. They'd managed to sell the posies quite quickly, before they'd wilted, and on the way back, they'd bought some fresh bread to go with the rabbit stew their mother had cooking over the fire. Not all days were as good, but the sisters were used to disappointment and took the bad days in their stride.

Once Margot left school she went straight to work at the silk factory where she was placed on the bobbins. She learnt to carefully adjust the speeds to make sure that she didn't ruin the material and though the work was hard, she enjoyed it.

She mixed with girls of her own age and when the supervisor wasn't watching they could quietly chat amongst themselves. If they were caught they'd get a stiff telling off and a warning that they were in danger of having money stopped from their pay. They'd wait until the supervisor had moved on, then giggle amongst themselves, careful not to attract his attention again.

The best thing about the job was that she had some wages to help her mum put food on the table. Her father quickly learnt what day she'd got paid, and would stand with one hand on his hip and the other palm reaching out.

"Hand it over." He'd demand and though Margot desperately wanted to disobey him, she would lower her head in shame, and slowly withdraw her envelope from her apron pocket.

The first time she'd tried asking, "Can't I keep a bit?"

Walter's response was to slap her soundly across the face, leaving a scarlet mark across her cheek. So the next time, as she left the factory, she secreted a small amount of the money out of her wage. Luckily Walter didn't notice and as soon as Margot could get her mother on her own she gave her the money.

"Where did you get this?" Her mother asked nervously.

"It's mine. I earnt it, ma. Go on, take it. Get us some bread, maybe a knob or two of butter."

"What if your father notices?" Mabel asked timidly.

"He won't. And if he does. Tell him you bought it cheap."

Mabel nodded and quickly grabbed the money out of Margot's hand and squirrelled it away.

The next day, Margot returned home to find a half

loaf of bread and some jam on the table. Mabel smiled at her daughter and Margot felt a sense of pride in being able to help her mother feed her sisters and brothers.

Each payday, Margot would find her father waiting for her and she'd meekly handover the small envelope with her meagre wages in. She would have to keep her head down as she did so because she knew that her eyes would be flashing in anger as she passed over the money. She'd always say a silent thank you that she'd managed to slip a little out to give her mother, before handing it over, and, if Walter did notice the envelope was a little light, Margot was lucky enough for him not to mention it.

"Look at me." Walter demanded on one occasion, as he noticed the defiant look on Margot's face.

Margot looked at up, biting her lip, so the words she wanted to say didn't accidentally slip out.

"You owe me." He told her. "I've fed and clothed you all your good for nothing life. Now it's time you to pay me back."

Margot nodded flatly, thinking, *That's on our ma, not you. You've drunk most of your wages, if mum hadn't been so frugal, we'd starved by now.*

At times like that she felt in total despair. *What is life all about, I get up, go to work, come back, help ma around the house, before going to sleep, ready to do exactly the same thing tomorrow,* she'd think.

Not that she begrudged helping her mother around the house and with her brothers and sisters, it's just she'd like to think that her life might be different one day. But for the time being at least, she was resigned to the fact that nothing was going to change. Insert chapter two text here.

CHAPTER THREE

" Come and get your fresh fish 'ere." Robert cried out loudly to the men and women passing by. Being a fishmonger meant that he had had to lose the natural reticence he'd learned growing up in the work house.

Robert was a tall brash man with a natural wave in his brown hair, that no amount of water could dampen down. With bushy eyebrows and a permanent frown, people could be guilty of looking on him unfavourably. Robert had grown up not knowing who his father was and mostly separated from his mother.

He had learned the hard way, not to show too many emotions especially once his mother disappeared when he was just eight years old. Just as he was dropping off to sleep he could still often hear the sharp voice from the workhouse, "You better stop crying before I give you summat to cry about."

As he got older, he'd been lucky enough to find a job with an old fishmonger out near billingsgate market, and had soon been able to leave the workhouse for a space on the fishmongers floor. Mr Harding had relied on Robert to get up early and bag the freshest fish of the morning. By the time he'd got to the stall, Robert had set up their daily produce and was ready to start selling to passersby.

It was Mr Harding who'd managed to drag Robert out of his shell, teaching him to sell to his customers, and even engage in a little banter as he did so. It didn't come naturally to Robert, who preferred to remain a little more aloof to the mostly female clientele.

That was until he'd met Mary. He'd fallen in love with her at first sight and when she smiled at him, he'd flushed red and struggled to get his words out. Eventually Robert had asked her out and she'd happily accepted saying, "I wondered how long it was going to take you." and laughing gently at him.

They'd got married not long after and had a beautiful baby girl. "She looks just like you." He'd murmured to

Mary, with a broad smile on his face.

"Nonsense," she'd reply. "She's all you. She's got that beautiful wave through her hair, just like yours."

They called her Anna and he loved her more deeply than he'd ever thought possible.

Robert had been so happy when Mary had told him that she was expecting again. Anna was getting older and he loved the idea of her having a little playmate. This time however, the pregnancy didn't go as well as the previous one. Mary's bump was so huge that it was uncomfortable for her to get out of bed, which meant that Robert needed someone to help out with Anna. Mary's sister Charlotte had agreed to visit and look after Anna and Mary, until the baby was born.

When Mary finally went into labour, Robert knew instantly that something was wrong. He ran for midwife and as soon as she arrived, she shouted to him, "I need hot water and towels. Get some blankets too."

She looked around at Robert who was just standing there in shock. "Come on man. Your wife needs you." She said sternly but kindly.

Robert ran to get the water and towels, while Charlotte pulled Anna out of the way. "What's the matter with ma?" Wailed Anna, seeing her mother was in pain, but not knowing what was happening.

Charlotte put her arms around the little girl and said, "She'll be fine, I promise. She's just getting ready to meet your little brother or sister, okay?"

Anna nodded, but the quiet sobs continued from underneath Charlotte's embrace.

An hour later, the midwife looked around. "It's a boy."

Robert rushed over to Mary's bedside.

She was dripping with sweat, and looked exhausted. "Is he okay?" She asked.

"He's grand." Replied the midwife. "Now if you don't mind, I'll be off."

Robert showed her out and then rushed back to where Charlotte and Anna were crowding around the bed.

"Let her be." He told them. "She needs her rest."

Charlotte nodded. "Give me the baby." She said. "I'll take good care of him, I promise."

Mary handed the boy over before falling exhausted into a deep sleep.

The next few weeks were difficult. Mary never really recovered from the birth so Charlotte persuaded her husband that she was needed there a little while longer.

She would prepare small meals for Mary, but Mary would push them away. "I'm not hungry." She'd say as Charlotte tried to persuade her to eat.

"Do it for the children's sake, if not for your own." Charlotte would tell her sternly.

When Robert came in from work he would go straight into see Mary who'd smile wanly at him, before falling back onto the pillows.

"How's she been today?" He'd whisper to Charlotte.

"No better, I'm afraid." She'd reply. "I'm so worried for her."

Robert nodded. "Me too. Do you think I should call the doctor?"

Charlotte thought for a moment. "It might be wise. It's been over a month now and she doesn't seem to be getting any stronger. Why don't you leave it until tomorrow morning and see how she is?"

Robert nodded and sat down to eat his dinner. He had a couple of mouthfuls before pushing it away.

"Not you too." Charlotte said. "Look, you need to

keep your strength up. For work and for your family."

Robert nodded but knew he couldn't stomach another mouthful. He pushed the food around for a few more minutes before giving up.

"I'd better get some kip." He told his sister-in-law.

"Yes, I'm feeling quite tired." Charlotte said.

"And if she's no better in the morning, we'll get the doctor out."

"Goodnight, Robert."Charlotte said gently, knowing how worried they both were about Mary.

But the next morning was too late. Mary had died during the night, leaving Robert and their two children alone. Robert wept until he could weep no more and then told himself stoically, "There's no point in crying over spilt milk. We just gotta make the best of it all."

Charlotte stayed for a while to look after the children, but she had her own children and needed to get back to them. She tried to persuade her husband to adopt the children, but he refused. Although Robert wondered if they might be better off with their aunt, he was secretly pleased that he wasn't going to lose his family.

CHAPTER FOUR

With the extra money that was coming in from Margot's wages, Walter started to gamble more heavily than ever before. He wasn't a smart man, and would often get hoodwinked by men working together and end up losing all his money. Wanting to win back his money he would borrow from the same person who'd won his money, until eventually the thrill of gambling took hold and he couldn't help spending more and more money trying to win bets against both friends and strangers.

The more he borrowed, the more difficult he found paying it back off, until he got himself in such debt he couldn't see his way out of it. Eventually someone threatened him with a debtors prison if he didn't pay up by the following week. Desperate to find a solution he looks around at how he might be able to raise some much needed capital. *It's either that or finding myself in gaol or one of those prison boats on its way to Australia,* he thought as he was leaving the factory one evening.

As he was walking along the street, he heard the street cries of the stall owners. Looking up he noticed the Robert, who he recognised as someone who lives in the street around the corner from his regular drinking hole. Walter looked at him thoughtfully. *He looks like he's doing all right for himself. Some people get all the luck,* Walter thought sneering at the fishmonger.

As he continued his way home, he smiled to himself as a plan started to emerge. Knowing the fishmonger lived alone after his wife's death, he decided that he was going to break into his home and see if there was anything worth robbing. *He's got more than me, and that's just not fair,* he said to himself, trying to justify his actions. *I'll do it tomorrow, just before dusk.*

The next evening as the night was drawing in, Walter found himself outside of Robert's house. He put his ear to the door and then looked through the window. There was no sign of anyone. Turning his head from side to side, to make sure he wasn't being watched, Walter forced open the door and slid quickly inside.

Walter was busy rummaging through the shelves and drawers, and failed to hear the door creak open behind him.

"What are you doing?" Robert demanded.

Walter froze, realising he'd been caught, he turned to face the man of the house.

"Please sir, please don't call the police. I'm sorry. I was just so desperate to feed my starving children." Walter said hoping that Robert would feel sympathetic towards him.

What Walter hadn't accounted for, what that Robert was familiar with him and his family as well as Walter's gambling problem. With a hard heart, he looked down his long nose at Walter and said, "That's not my problem. It's up to you to pay your way. You've tried to steal from me and now it's time for you to get your comeuppance."

Walter's heart sank. If he didn't go to gaol for breaking in, he would surely end up in debtors prison. Either way it didn't look good for him. Thinking quickly he smiled. Robert looked at him suspiciously. This didn't look like a man who was just about to have the police called for him.

"What are you smiling about?" Robert demanded.

"You lost your wife a little while ago, didn't you? Walter asked.

Robert looked him with furrowed brow. He couldn't believe this man had the gall to even mention his wife.

"What's that got to do with anything?" He said angrily.

"Well," said, Walter, "I have a daughter, well I've got more than one actually, but the one I'm referring to is eighteen. She's a little younger than you, but she has six younger siblings and she's used to looking after them, so she could live here with you and take care of your children?"

Robert looked at Walter as though he had lost his mind. "You'd use your daughter to get out of going to prison?"

Walter looked at Robert and smirked. "No. I'd expect you to pay off my debts too."

Robert looked at him. *Is this man really saying he'd sell his daughter to get himself out of trouble!* He thought, horrified that such a man could exist.

Then he looked again at Walter. *Maybe she'd be better off away from him anyway*, he thought. *And the neighbours are starting to get a little tired of my reliance on them. Anna and Alfie need stability. It's so difficult without Mary. I don't want them having to grow up like me, not being able to show them how much I care about them. But I can't stay at home. Without my income, we'd be on the streets. Maybe his daughter could be the answer to both our problems.*

Walter watched as he could see that Robert was split between what he thought was right and what would make his life easier. His smiled widened as he saw Robert's resolve melting away.

"And how do I know that you wouldn't renege on your promise?" Robert asked Walter.

"You got my word." He replied.

"I'm not sure that means much." Replied Robert dubiously.

Walter tried to look indignant, but knew that Robert had got a handle on his character.

"Why don't I leave now, tell my daughter what we've agreed and then she can move in as soon as possible, afore you give me the money for me debts. What say you?"

Robert stroked his chin as he thought it through.

"Okay. That works for me." He eventually replied.

"So, I'm free to go?" Asked Walter.

"Yes," said Robert. "I suppose so, but you've got until Monday to bring your daughter to meet me, otherwise I'll be telling the police on you."

"Monday it is." Replied Walter as he strode across the room to the front door, pushing it open and quickly disappearing into the night.

Walter gave a huge sigh of relief as he turned the corner onto his street. The sense of relief didn't last long, when he realised that he was going to have to give up her wages. *Well, better that than prison, I suppose.* He thought pragmatically.

As Robert started preparing the dinner in advance of the children coming through the door, the enormity of the agreement he'd just made came over him. He sunk down into the nearest chair. *What have I done?* He thought. *What will people say about a young girl setting up home here, with us? I didn't think this through.*

He was still sat there worrying about his decision when Anna and Alfie turned up ten minutes later.

"You all right pa?" Asked Anna, carrying Alfie over to the bed, near where their father was sitting.

Robert smiled at them both. "Never better." He said, deciding that tomorrow would be soon enough to tell them of their change in circumstance.

CHAPTER FIVE

Walter decided to go straight home and share the good news. *One less mouth to feed*, he thought as he strutted down the street toward his home. He pushed open the door and filled the whole door way as he stood there looking around at his family.

Margot looked at him suspiciously. *What's he in such a good mood for?* She thought. *I can't remember the last time he arrived home in a good mood, in fact, he seems to have got worse and worse lately. What could it be?*

Walter plonked himself down and looked over at Margot. "Get 'ere." He demanded.

Wondering what she might have done wrong,

Margot unwillingly turned from the sink, where she was preparing the vegetables for their tea and scuttled over to her father.

Try not to start anything while he's in a good mood, she thought.

"Yes Pa, what is it you want?" she asked as meekly as she could manage.

Walter looked at his eldest child and smirked. "I've only gone and got you a new job." He told her.

Margot was flabbergasted, "You done what?" she asked.

A black look flashed across Walter's face and Margot instinctively shrank back slightly, even though she berated herself for feeling so scared.

"I said, I got you a new job."

"But I already got a job and I like it perfectly well." Margot said, still bewildered by the conversation.

Walter sneered, "This new job be a live-in position. All your bed and board paid for." He said, forgetting to mention that it wasn't actually a paid position, but that she'd be working to pay off his debts.

"But Ma needs me here, don't you Ma?" She asked turning towards Mabel.

But Mabel was too scared to intervene and studiously ignored her daughter, while at the same time worrying about how she was going to manage without Margot's help.

"What if I refuse?" Margot demanded, rather more bravely than she was feeling.

"You'll do as I say, or you'll find yourself on the streets." Her father warned her

"Please, Father, don't make me do this." She begged.

But her pleas fell on deaf ears. Walter's good mood had totally disappeared with the exasperation he was feeling towards his eldest girl. In a low and mean voice he said, "I told him we'd go round his on Monday and you can meet your new employer and that's what we're going to do. Do you understand me girl."

Margot knew there was nothing she could do or say to change her father's mind, so she sullenly nodded her head and went back to preparing the vegetables. While she was peeling the potatoes, she wondered whether she would be better off running away but then reality stuck. *Where would I run? Where would I go? I've nowhere to go. I've got no choice,* she thought, resigning herself to the fact that her life would soon be changing.

The next morning Robert sat his young daughter down and explained that there was going to be a nice lady who was coming to live with them and would be there to take care of Anna and her baby brother. Anna had lots of questions about the new lady and Robert realised that he knew nothing of Margot, except for her name.

Am I really doing the right thing for my children, bringing in a stranger to look after them? What if they don't like her? What if she is cruel to them, after all, she is the daughter to that awful dullard. Oh, why did I let him persuade me, he thought, as he started to regret not calling the police instead of agreeing to this unusual arrangement.

CHAPTER SIX

Monday came and Margot went reluctantly along with her father to meet Robert. Walter tapped confidently at the door, happy that he found a solution to his money worries. *I might even be able to milk the situation further down the line*, he thought.

Robert opened the door tentatively and poked his head through a small gap.

"I'm not sure about this." He admitted to the man standing in front of him.

"We shook on it." Replied Walter sternly. "You can't go back on the deal now." He warned, putting his hand towards the door.

Robert nodded, as a man of honour he didn't

contemplate pushing the debate any further.

"You'd better come in then." As he opened the door wider.

Walter shoved Margot through the doorway and into the small room. Margot looked around curiously. The house was bigger than her parents home, *and only three of them living 'ere,* she thought.

Although the room was quite big it was quite dark and had a slight aroma to it that she wasn't used to. *Bit of damp maybe, be all right once I've given it a clean, I 'spect*, she thought. There were two beds, opposite each other and a small table against one of the walls which were painted in a sage green. It might have been nice once, but it was now showing signs of neglect. *I wonder where I'll be expected to sleep?* She thought nervously.

She smiled shyly at the man in front of her, who was a bit older than her, but not as old as she'd been expecting. He was tall and broad shouldered, with brown hair that he pushed back off his face and deep brown eyes that seemed to pierce her soul.

Robert noticed her looking.

"You must be Margot." He said in an unemotional

voice.

Margot looked at him in surprise. She wasn't sure why he was so grumpy. *He'd been the one to offer the position, wasn't he?* She thought.

Rather than say anything that might upset either her father, or this man, she gave a half smile and dipped her knee slightly before answering "Yes, sir. I'm Margot."

"And you've got experience of young children?" He demanded.

"Why yes, sir. I help my mother with my six younger brother and sisters, the youngest of which is only three years old sir."

"Very good." Robert responded. "Now if you are to live here you will have to stop calling me sir."

Margot looked up at him in confusion.

"I haven't been told your name, sir."

Robert looked puzzled and looked over her head at her father.

"I wasn't sure what you'd want her to call you." Explained Walter dismissively.

Robert looked back at Margot and said, "If you're going to be living here, you'd better call me Robert, I suppose. Does that suit?"

"Yes Sir, I mean Robert." Stammered Margot nervously.

Behind her Walter gave a harsh laugh. "You stupid girl. Just call him by his name and be done with it. Now. When do you want her to start?" He asked, turning to Robert.

Robert pondered for a moment and replied, "What about next weekend, give 'er time to say 'er goodbyes?"

"Sounds good to me." Replied Walter.

"And you?" Robert asked Margot.

"Spose." Replied Margot nodding. "Got t' give notice to the silk factory. Be end of week afore I finish, so Sunday is okay."

The men nodded at each other and then, much to Robert's consternation, Walter grabbed Margot harshly by the arm and said, "Best be off then. I'll send 'er round Sunday, just after breakfast."

Margot looked back at Robert as she was dragged out of the room. "Good bye... Robert."

"Good bye," replied Robert grateful to see the back of them.

It wasn't until they were walking back that Margot realised she hadn't met the children. *I wonder where they were?* She thought. *I hope they know I'm coming.*

Sunday came around quickly and Margot woke early with butterflies in her stomach. *What if they don't like me. What if I don't like them. Oh no, this is going to be a nightmare.*

The thoughts swirled around in her head, making her more and more nervous, until she decided that the best thing to do would be to get up and start packing her small amount of belongings, before starting to prepare breakfast.

After breakfast she pulled her brothers and sisters into a small circle around her and told them she was off.

"But, why are you going away?" Asked one.

"I don't want you to go." Said another.

The youngest started crying, not really knowing what was going on, but picking up on the distress that was emanating from the others.

Margot tried hard to hold back the tears.

"I don't want to go either, but I must. I'm going to be looking after a couple of children just like you, and I won't be too far away. I'll come to visit as often as I can and in the meantime Lucy will take care of you, along with mother."

Lucy smiled at the younger ones.

"I promise to look after you just like Margot does." She told them.

One of them grabbed Margot's skirts to try and stop her from leaving, but Margot bent down and gently peeled back her fingers.

"I'm sorry, my lovelies. I've got to go. I'll see you soon."

Walter heard her make her promise and stood up sharply.

"You will not see them soon. I don't want you back and forth. No my girl, you be off now and I don't want to see you 'ere again."

Margot looked at him in shock.

"But Da." Margot said the tears flooding down her cheeks. "You can't stop me from visiting my family."

Walter towered over her threateningly.

"You wanna bet on that?" He demanded angrily.

"You come back 'ere any time soon and you'll get the back of me 'and. Is that clear?"

Margot looked up at him, and knew he was telling it as it was. "Yes Da." She said eventually, once she'd managed to hold back her sobs.

She picked up her pillow cases and gave the little ones one last kiss before standing up tall and walking towards the front door.

"Bye Ma. Look after yourself. Good bye Lucy, I love you all." She said sorrowfully as she took one last look at them and left the house on to her new life.

It didn't take long for Margot to reach Robert's house and as she arrived, she saw two young children sat on the door step to the house.

"You must be Anna and Alfie?" She asked. "I'm Margot."

"Nice to meet you." Replied Anna shyly.

"Is your father home?" Margot asked nervously.

"Our father is waiting for you inside." Said Anna.

Margot tapped on the door, which was quickly opened by Robert, who looked as nervous as she did. He called the children in and introduced them formally to one another. He then pointed out the bed that Margot would be sharing with the children.

Margot felt a huge sense of relief that she'd be

sleeping with Anna and Alfie, as she hadn't really been sure what her father had agreed with Robert.

Robert must have noticed the relief on Margot's face and asked brusquely, "What did you father tell you about the setup here?"

"Nothing sir."replied Margot.

"Robert." He retorted quickly.

"Sorry, Si, I mean Robert." Margot said, feeling scared that she was going straight from the frying pan into the fire.

Robert explained her duties to her, "Your main job is to look after the children. Anna will need to be taken to school. I might need you at times to help on the stall and I know the house isn't as tidy as it could be. Since my wife's death, I've not had anyone in to do it, so you will need to spend some time getting it in order."

Margot nodded.

"And I will expect you to prepare breakfast before I leave in the morning and for dinner to be on the table by the time I get home. Otherwise there will be consequences Do you understand?"

Margot looked him meekly and nodded.

Robert turned away, leaving her to looking after him

open-mouthed with shock at how suddenly her life had changed.

CHAPTER SEVEN

Margot was washing the dishes after a long day. She wiped her hair away from her face and sighed quietly. She knew better than to attract Robert's attention. If he thought she was bemoaning her fate, he would snap at her.

"Your father got you into this not me, so don't you be complaining, you hear me?" Margot would silently respond, thinking, *Yes, but Da never told me I'd be working for nothing. I'm worse off than I was at the factory. I can't even give Ma any money for food now*, but she never responded, knowing her father would smack her senseless if she were to return home.

Not that Robert treated her badly. *No, I've not got a beating since I left home. I hope Lucy isn't copping it too much, now I'm not there to take the brunt,* she said to herself as her thoughts turned to her family. *I wish I could see them, but Father forbade me to do so, and I don't want to make life more difficult for Ma and Lucy.*

She had settled into life with Robert and the children. Anna was a shy and timid girl, whom Margot had come to love. She had pale blue eyes and thin blonde hair. Short for her age with porcelain skin, she made Margot feel quite protective of the little girl.

Her brother Alfie was much more boisterous. He had chubby rosy cheeks and pudgy little legs that wobbled as he weaved across the room as fast as he could. He had a ready smile and loved to come up onto Margot's lap for a snuggle before going down to sleep. The children were delightful and if it hadn't been for their father, she would have loved living there.

However, it seemed that Robert hadn't taken to her. In fact he was always quite gruff towards her. She got up every day, so that she could give him breakfast before he left to get to the market for five o'clock each morning.

When she'd asked him why he got there so early, he would grunt at her and then say in a tone that suggested she should already know the answer to her question, "I need to make sure I get the best fish, before the costermongers take 'em all for themselves."

While he was at work Margot walked Anna to school before coming back to clean the house, making sure that it was spotless ready for his return. He gave her a measly allowance in which to keep the children clothed and food on the table. But Margot did her best to make sure that none of them went hungry.

And from time to time she was expected to cover the stall. Taking Alfie with her, she would do her best to keep an eye on the toddler as well as the customers, but at times, Robert would reproach her for ignoring their regulars.

"Can't you keep a better eye on him. Why do you let him run around like that? He's putting off the customers. You need to be more strict with him" He told her one occasion when Alfie decided that he'd had enough of sitting on the blanket that Margot had put down for him to play on. *Easy for him to say*, she thought, *doesn't he remember being that age?*

Robert was kind to the children, but did expect them to be seen and not heard, so Margot would try to make sure they were quiet and kept out of their father's way when he got home tired from work. Luckily Anna often wanted to practice her letters and handing over a crayon to Alfie to draw on a scrap of paper, could keep him occupied for hours, most of the time.

Through all of this, what made Margot quite cross was that Robert didn't seem to feel any gratitude for the effort she was making. *He could say thank you occasionally,* she thought one evening as she was folding some clothes to put away tidily. *In fact, he doesn't really talk at all, unless it's to complain about something. 'The children are too loud. Why isn't dinner on the table when I come in? The house is a mess.' I wish he had one good word to say about my work here.*

But Margot knew she wouldn't say anything. She'd just nod at him when he made those comments and tell him she'd do better next time. She didn't think he was the kind of man to beat her, but she didn't want to give him any excuse to do so.

CHAPTER EIGHT

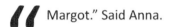 Margot." Said Anna.

"Yes, Anna?" She replied.

"Do we really have to have a bath today, we had one a couple of days ago."

Margot laughed, remembering how dirty the children were when she arrived. In fact she'd made bathing them one of her first tasks.

"That was only a sponge bath." Margot reminded Anna. "And you got yourself all dirty when you fell over in the market, remember?"

"Oh, but..." Anna tried.

"But nothing." Margot said smiling. "Come on, I'll brush your hair after for you."

Anna reluctantly got in the bath with her brother, who was happily splashing and blowing bubbles in the tin bath in front of the fire.

Margot passed her the soap, "Don't forget to wash behind your ears." She said as she turned away from the bath to go fetch clean clothes for the two children to put on once they'd finished.

Margot felt it was important for the children to keep clean. Her mother had always told her that dirty children picked up germs easier, and she didn't want either Anna or Alfie getting sick. Each morning she would put a comb through their hair, before setting off to take Anna to school.

"I could walk on my own, it's not far." Said Anna one morning.

"I know you could." Replied Margot gently. "But I like the walk and it's good for Alfie to get some fresh air. Anyway, don't you like us waving you goodbye as you enter the school building?"

Anna blushed and smiled, "Yes, it makes me feel happy."

"Then let's not say any more about it. We'll walk you to school every morning, until you decide you don't want me to. Agreed?"

"Agreed." Smiled Anna as she bent down over her handwriting practice and continued her studies.

Margot looked at the top of Anna's head and smiled. The more time she spent with them, the closer she felt to them. They were both such different characters.

Even though Anna was the quiet shy one, she was clumsy and would often bump into things as she wandered through town. Margot would gently tell her to get her head out the clouds, and Anna would blush with embarrassment that someone might laugh at her lack of grace.

Alfie was louder and a bit of a whirlwind at times, but he seemed to go through life without incident. Margot hoped that would always be the case for the darling boy, she was starting to love as if he were her own.

It's not like their father gives them a lot of affection, she thought. He is kindly with them, but they need more that that. Without their mother they need someone to comfort them when they have a bad day, and encourage them to get on with things.

The more Margot filled this void, the closer the

children got to her. As she was pulling Alice's hair into a bun, she turned round to look over her shoulder at Margot.

"You won't leave us, will you Margot?" She asked.

Margot stopped in her tracks. She didn't really know what the agreement was between her father and Robert, so she wasn't sure how long she'd be there. *What should I say?* She thought.

Bending her knees so that she was at the same level as the little girl, Margot held Anna by her shoulders.

"Anna, Wherever I am and whatever I do, I promise I will always be there for you. If you need me, you will just have to ask."

She smiled softly at the young girl, who'd lost her mother way too early, then pulled her into her arms for a huge hug. Alfie didn't know what was going on, but he loved having cuddles, so he tumbled over to the two of them and stretched out his arms. Margot and Anna looked at him, then looked back at each other and laughed.

"Come here." Margot said, scooping Alfie up in her arms and bringing him into the fold.

Later that night, as Robert even smiled as he sat

down to eat, Margot thought, maybe life isn't so bad..

CHAPTER NINE

Margot heard a sharp tap on the door. She turned around surprised. It wasn't something that happened very often. She put down her cloth and smoothed down her apron before answering the door. It was an elderly woman with a few butchered rabbits tied together with string.

"Good morning my dear, I've got these for sale, You want a couple?"

Margot looked at them thoughtfully. They would make a nice change. Her brow furrowed as she looked at the woman in front of her.

"Where did you get them?" She asked suspiciously. There was no way this elderly lady could have shot them herself.

"My husband caught 'em, so 'e did." The woman said with a toothless smile. "They're fresh enough and very cheap."

Margot looked at the costermonger, then again at the rabbits. Although the woman looked as though she could do with a wash, the rabbits smelt okay and once I've cleaned them, they'd probably make a nice stew, she thought.

"But I've never actually skinned a rabbit before. Is it difficult?"

The woman laughed.

"If you buy one, I'll show how to skin it so you know how to for next time. How's that for a deal?"

Margot smiled, and nodded. "Okay, you got yourself a deal."

She paid the costermonger and she quickly skinned it, before going on to the next door.

Margot smiled as she shut the door and turned towards the hearth. She chopped it into rough chunks, along with some vegetables and put them all in the pot to cook through. She smiled as she stirred the stew, thinking *I hope Robert appreciates the effort*, as the air filled with the delicious aromas of the earthy and flavoursome stew.

As Margot dished out the stew to Robert and the children, he looked up at her and frowned.

"What have we 'ere?"

"It's rabbit stew." Margot replied nervously. "I thought it would make a change from fish. Why? Don't you like it?"

Roberts face darkened with anger.

"That's not the point. We've not got money to throw around. I give you a good allowance and when it's gone it's gone, Don't you be thinking you can get some more at the end of the week if you run out."

"But it were cheap." Margot explained. "I got it off a costermonger who was touting her wares round 'ere."

"Probably stolen then." Robert said angrily as he stood up, pushing his chair back.

"And when did you decide that fish wasn't good enough for you? What, you too high and mighty for fish?"

Margot spluttered trying to explain that that wasn't what she'd meant, but Robert stormed off, leaving Margot and the two children sat there looking bewildered.

"He won't make you leave, will he?" Asked Anna, scared that she was going to lose her friend and protector.

"Of course not." Replied Margot, not wanting to upset the children but not knowing if what she was saying was true. *I hope not anyway*, she thought as she pulled Anna in for a hug.

He marched up the road in a dreadful temper, then as he anger dissipated, Robert's step became to slow. *What was I even cross about? The stew did smell tasty and who am I to tell her how to manage her allowance, she's managed okay so far. I'd better apologise when I get back,* he thought embarrassed at his outburst.

Margot was sat sewing when he returned. She'd been thinking of her previous working life at the factory. *I really miss having friends to natter with, and ask what they think about things, such as this argument with Robert. I wonder what it was all about?*

Robert stood in front of Margot.

"I'm sorry." He said.

"Do you not like rabbit? Margot asked, "'cos I can make sure I never cook it again, if you don't"

"It's not that. I do like rabbit. I just had a bad day,

that's all. It won't happen again."

Margot looked up at him and smiled sweetly.

"Okay." She said as she continued repairing the dress that Anna had ripped on a fence on the way home from school.

CHAPTER TEN

Robert had started to rely more on Margot and she spent a greater proportion of her time helping out on the stall. She still had to take Alfie with her, but he had learned not to run off and when he did the other market owners would catch hold of him and bring him back, usually with a small treat to keep him occupied throughout the day.

While Margot helping out one day, Robert left her minding the stall while he made a return trip to Billingsgate market to purchase some more fish. They had already sold more than they'd expected, so he was hopeful that the day was going to be a good one.

Margot had started to enjoy helping out at the market. She enjoyed chatting to the other market stall owners and the customers would often want a natter, before moving on to the next stall. It felt like life had finally turned a corner, and she was enjoying having a bit more freedom than she'd managed while living with her parents.

As Robert returned, he noticed Margot talking to one of the other stallholders. She was laughing at something he'd said and Robert couldn't help notice the flush of happiness on her cheeks. He stopped for a moment and watched the two mid conversation.

The man she was talking to was a younger man and according to some of Robert's female customer was really quite handsome. Robert had seen him around more than once flirting with the women who came shopping at his stall.

Next thing he knew he was storming over there.

"Stop your chatting and get on with your work. Can't you see you are losing customers." He barked at her.

With a flash of anger, Margot turned suddenly, shocked at Robert's outburst.

"I've been busy all morning. We've had a little lull and so I was just chatting to Marcus here." She said sharply.

Robert replied. "I don't pay you to chat."

Margot put her hand on her chest and took a sharp intake of breath.

"You don't pay me at all. I'm doing this because of an agreement between you and my father."

Robert looked abashed, but swallowed his embarrassment and continued to verbally attack Margot.

"Well, you're going to get a name for yourself if you start spending time with people like that."

Margot looked at him horrified, she'd just been having a little bit of banter with Marcus, like she did with all the other stallholders. *Just because he doesn't like to chat with the others, don't mean I shouldn't,* she thought. *It don't make me a bad person.*

Looking around, she noticed that Marcus had left sometime during the argument, probably didn't want to get involved in this spat that Robert has started for no reason whatsoever, she thought angrily.

She looked at him shocked, with tears threatening. She snatched up Alfie and stormed off, leaving Robert standing openmouthed behind her. *When did she get so impertinent,* he thought to himself.

As Robert watched her leave, he closed his eyes and grimaced. *What was I thinking, I had no right to have shout at her for chatting to another man. She looked really happy.She's still quite young, really. Maybe she'd be better off without me and the children.* He wondered. His thoughts turned to him and his family's needs. Margot was such a great help, to all three of them. *We need her and it was her father that arranged it's so she'll have to put up with it.*

As Margot marched back to Roberts house she started to calm down. *I can't live like this I need to get out there, but what would happen to Anna and Alfie, they need me. I'm not sure I could leave them alone. I think I'll sleep on it, and decide what to do in the morning. Maybe Robert will apologise and things will settle down.*

When Robert finally arrived home, Margot knew straight away that he hadn't changed his opinion. He struggled to look at her and when she set the dinner on the table, he grunted and then shovelled in his food as if to get away from her as quick as possible.

Margot was disappointed, but knew that he had forced her to think very carefully about her future.

CHAPTER ELEVEN

When Margot woke up she had made a decision. She knew that she could no longer live with the situation. It was bad enough that her father manipulated her so much, but being controlled by a man who meant nothing to her was another matter. *No, I'm going to tell him that I'm packing my bags and leaving,* she decided as she was preparing breakfast.

Robert was still in a bad mood when he arrived at the table. Margot tried to broach the subject of leaving, but when she went to open her mouth, her words dried up. Her stomach was in knots, worrying about his reaction to her decision. She didn't realise that Robert was feeling ashamed of his outburst, the day before, but didn't want to acknowledge any weakness. He was a proud man and never liked to admit if he were in the wrong.

"Maybe we should talk later? He asked as he picked up his coat to leave.

"That's a good idea." Replied Margot.

She hoped that he was going to say that it wasn't working out and that he wanted her to go. *It would save a lot of worry*, she thought as she went about her housework. As she swept through, then scrubbed the floor, she became more and more convinced that leaving was the right thing to do.

She missed her family dreadfully, and was worried how Father was treating them now she wasn't there to protect them. I wish I'd been brave enough to visit them and see for myself, rather than rely on the small titbits I pickup at the market, she thought, standing up to wring out her cloth once more.

Alfie picked up on her disquiet which put him in a temper too. Every so often he would lift his arms to Margot and say, "Cuddles." Margot smiled as she picked him up for a cradle before setting him down again. She knew it was going to be difficult to leave them, but leave them is what she must do.

When Robert returned from the market, Margot made sure the dinner was ready. She put the food on the table, and then took a deep breath, plucking up the courage to say what was on her mind. As Robert was sat there with his spoon in his hand, Margot looked directly at him.

"I need to say something." She said more confidently than she was feeling.

Robert looked up at her surprised. Usually Margot was demure and rarely started a conversation. He'd not seen this bolder side of her personality.

"What about?" He asked.

"I'm leaving." She told him, "I need to return back to my family. I miss them dreadfully."

Robert gave a harsh laugh. "I'm sure you do. You've not even visited them since you been 'ere."

"But" said Margot trying to interrupt him and explain that her father had forbidden her todo so. "But nothing." Robert continued. "This has nothing to do with your family. This is about that man you were talking to on the market. Well I'm afraid that you're going to have to change your plans. Your father exchanged you in return for paying 'is debts and so I wouldn't call the police on 'is thieving. You'll stay 'ere until I don't need you anymore. Do you understand?"

Margot looked at him in shock. She didn't realise what a temper he had.

"You wouldn't really make me stay, would you?" She pleaded.

But Robert was incensed. He took umbrage at the way she seemed so quickly to forget her commitment to the children and what he saw as a total disrespect for him and his feelings.

"And anyway, no one's going to want you now, not now you've been living with me for the last few months. They'll assume that you've been my mistress, and they won't touch you with a barge pole."

Margot looked at Robert horrified. She hadn't even thought about the consequences of living with a single man, even with the children here. *How naive am I!* She thought.

"I've been sleeping with the kids." She said.

"But no one knows that apart from you and I. Nobody will believe it. And if you leave. I will tell everybody that you're nothing more than a floozy."

Margot didn't know what else to say. She stood there

in shock for a moment before running weeping, from the table. She sat heavily on the edge of the bed with her head in her hands, not knowing what to do with herself.

In the hullabaloo, both Robert and Margot had forgotten that the children were there, not really understanding what was going on. Anna and Alfie could see how distressed Margot was and wanted to go and comfort her, but they'd never seen their father so angry. They sat as quiet as two church mice, hoping that he wouldn't turn his temper towards them.

As soon as they could the children tiptoed off to bed and crept silently in, cuddling up closely to Margot, whose sobs had turned to quiet weeping. Robert watched them go, cursing himself at the situation in which he found himself.

CHAPTER TWELVE

The next morning, Margot got up as usual and prepared breakfast, which Robert ate without once looking at her. Once he'd finished, he got up and grabbed his coat.

"Come on Anna, you're coming with me."

Anna looked at him bewildered, but did as she was told.

"What are you doing?" Margot asked.

"I'll ask a neighbour to mind 'er until it's time for her to go to school. You will stay here and to make sure you don't go anywhere, I'll be locking you in."

Margot looked at him horrified.

"You can't do that." She said quietly, not wanting to

upset the children any more than they already were.

"I can, and I'm going to." He replied, "I'm not letting you run off. You're needed here. Who would look after the children if not you?"

"What if I promise not to leave?" Margot cried.

"I don't trust you not to disappear as soon as I'm gone, leaving Alfie 'ere to cope on 'is own."

Margot couldn't believe what she was hearing.

"You have that low opinion of me?" She said tearfully.

Robert didn't reply, he just grabbed Anna by the arm and pulled her out of the door, slamming it shut behind him and locking the door. Margot tried the door to check that it was locked, and turned to lean against the door as she realised she was trapped.

She slowly walked over to the table and sat down. Alfie came over and grabbed her knees. She smiled gently at him, but swatted his hands away. She needed to think about what had just happened. Alfie tried to persist but could see that Margot wasn't having any of it, so he turned and started playing with some blocks Robert had picked up at the market for him.

Through the day, Robert starts to think about the

argument he'd provoked with Margot.

What have I done? She didn't deserve that. Why am I being like this. Why does she make me so crazy? She's really good with the kids. Maybe that's it? He asked himself, knowing there was more to it than that. *I can't have feelings for her, can I? No, it's not possible. I still love my wife and I hardly know this girl, and anyway, she's only with us because her father gave her no choice. I'm sure that she'll just leave as soon as she gets the chance, in fact she proved that today, but did I need to be so mean to her, no wonder she wants to leave. What am I going to do?*

A couple of the other stall holders tried to make conversation with him throughout the day, but Robert kept his head down and just grunted if someone asked him a question. Even his customers noticed his dour mood. When Mrs Baker came to get her usual herrings, she asked, "What's got into you?"

"Nothing." Replied Robert gruffly.

"Could 'ave fooled me." She replied. "Girl trouble, no doubt." She said smiling.

"Why, what you 'erd?" Robert more sharply than he usually would to a customer.

"Nothing." Mrs Baker replied quickly.

"Well, 'ere's your herring. Good day to you Mrs Baker." Robert said, making sure she knew that the conversation was over. Bet she goes around telling everyone how rude I was to her, the old flibbertigibbet! He thought meanly.

His thoughts continued to go round and round in circles until it was time to pack up for the day. As he slowly walked home, he reminded himself of why he'd done it and tried to persuade himself that what he'd done was for the best, but deep inside his stomach he had a knot that kept getting stronger, making him feel quite ill.

Arriving home, Robert pulled off his coat and sat down wearily. It hadn't been that busy, but with everything on his mind, he felt absolutely shattered. Margot quietly put his plate in front of him and dished up some of the broth she'd made. Robert looked at her, not knowing what to say or how to make things better. He picked up his spoon and started eating his meal.

Margot turned her back towards the fireplace again. She didn't want to eat with him. She despised him so much, but she knew she had to ask him what was on her mind. She dished herself out some broth before

65

sitting opposite Robert. She took a deep breath.

"About tomorrow, will I be taking Anna to school." She asked as politely as she could manage.

Robert's spoon paused as he was lifting it to him mouth. "No, I don't think so. I'll get the neighbour to do it again."

Margot could feel the tears well up behind her eyes. "You can't keep me locked up in here forever."

Robert didn't respond, so Margot tried again.

"We're going to need some groceries for tomorrow. Otherwise we won't eat."

"Fine." Responded Robert gruffly. "I'll bring some home. You'll have to just make do, until I return."

Margot looked at him in disbelief. Something surely had to change?

"Aren't you going to finish you meal?" He asked.

"I don't have much of an appetite." She responded defiantly.

"Well 'and it 'ere. I don't want good grub going to waste."

Margot sullenly handed over her plate and he scraped her food in with his own and continued to eat.

How can he pretend that none of this is happening, she thought. "Doesn't he care at all how I feel?

During the evening the atmosphere in the house grew worse. The children could feel the tension and didn't know what to say. They sat quietly not knowing what to do for the best. Margot looked at them. They'd hardly eaten anything either, so she moved to Alfie's side and picked up his spoon.

"Come on, let me help you. You won't grow big and strong like your sister if you don't eat."

As she talked quietly to the children about their days, she studiously ignored Robert, who now had his head in the penny paper he'd picked up on the way home. As soon as it was time for the children to go to bed, she clambered in with them. *I'm not spending any more time with that man than I have to,* she thought as she shut her eyes, trying to shut out the problem her current situation left her in.

CHAPTER THIRTEEN

I t had been a few days since Margot had been out of the house and it was starting to get her down. The only people she'd seen were Robert and the children, and the two adults were no longer on speaking terms, unless it was to do with the children.

Both Anna and Alfie had become more withdrawn as they noticed the hostility between Margot and their father. Margot had tried to reassure them, but the atmosphere in the house was quite subdued. Margot was anxious about her family.

When she'd been going out to take Anna to school on a daily basis, she'd been able to pick up titbits about her sister and mother, but now she didn't know if and when she would ever be able to go out again.

What if they're not coping without me, she thought. *What if he's taking it out on the younger ones. What would I do? It would all be my fault.* Alfie tried to get her attention, but Margot was too distressed to notice. Eventually Alfie realised that whatever he did wasn't working and went off to do his own thing. Margot sat at the small table with her head in her hands as she thought about her family and their situation.

Not being able to see a way out, she began to sob. She couldn't stand it anymore. She needed to see them, but she couldn't see any way of doing so. Robert wasn't going to let her out any time soon, and even if she did get out, her father would beat her if he found out she had visited.

Alfie played quietly in the corner, oblivious as only a child can be that anything was wrong with Margot. She was still sobbing hard as Robert returned home from work, pushing the door open and striding into the small room.

"What the hells wrong with you?" he said harshly, assuming that Margot was just thinking of her self and pining for her stall-holder.

As he heard the bitter tone in his voice, he realised that he'd been jealous. *Oh*, he thought, as he closed his eyes and trying to push down his emotions. *Is that the reason why I've been so mean? I'm upset that she might want somebody other than me?* Even though he knew he was in the wrong, he just couldn't help himself continue in the same vein.

"Haven't you started on the dinner yet," He asked sharply.

"Or are you too busy worrying about what your boyfriend is doing to care about feeding my children."

Margot looked at him with tears rolling down her face.

"What are you talking about?" She asked confused at what Robert had just said. "I'm worried about Lucy, and my mother." She said.

"Whatever for?" He asked. It was his turn to look confused.

"With me not there to take the brunt of the beatings, I don't know what'll 'appen."

Robert looked stunned.

"Are you telling me that your father used to beat on you?"

Margot nodded. The sobs had turned to quiet intakes of breath as she started to explain.

"He always used to beat Ma, then as I grew older he would sometimes turn to me. I was stronger than Ma, so I would try to get in the way if he started on her, and I used to make sure he didn't hit the younger ones."

Robert could feel the tears welling up in his eyes as he realised what a truly awful life she'd had growing up. Margot continued.

And now that I'm gone, Lucy will be the one he'll turn to and she's not as strong as me. She may not be able to protect the younger ones, like what I did."

Robert looked horrified as he realised how selfish he'd been, thinking of himself and assuming that Margot was looking to go off with another man, when in reality she was thinking of her family. He knelt beside her and handed his cleanish handkerchief.

"What can I do to help?" He asked. "There must be something." He said softly.

Margot looked up at him. This wasn't the Robert that she was beginning to get used to. She could see by the tears in his eyes that he cared about what she'd just told him.

"I'm not sure I'm not sure there's anything anybody can do." She said as she used the handkerchief to dry her eyes.

Robert helped her up and pulled a chair towards her. Sitting her down, he grabbed another spare chair.

"Tell me all about it, and we'll see what we can do." He said gently.

Margot took a deep breath. She'd never shared the whole truth with anyone. But there was something about Robert, that made her think that he might be able to make things better. He had a quiet strength about him and he didn't seem afraid to stand up for what he thought was right.

She started to tell Robert about her life grownup and once she started the floodgates open and she couldn't stop telling him everything. How her father used to spend all the money on ale, then return home drunk, taking his anger and frustrations on his children.

Robert listened as she unburdened herself. Once she'd exhausted herself, he looked at her shocked. He thought his early life had been hard, but it was nothing compared to what Margot had suffered under her father, and at least he'd met Mr Harding relatively early in life, so he didn't remember much of life in the workhouse.

"But that's not fair." He said, "You're just children."

Margot looked at him with a look that seemed too mature for her years.

"That doesn't seem to matter to our father." She told him, matter of factly.

Robert looked her in a new light. Margot was such a strong young woman, and however much her father may have tried to beat out of her. There was nothing he could do to quench her spirit and Robert was going to do his best to make sure no one ever tried to again.

CHAPTER FOURTEEN

Robert had been thinking about Margot's situation all day. The more he thought about it the more unfair it seemed. He didn't like the thought of her being beaten and worried about the fact that now someone else was taking the brunt. *It just isn't right*, he thought.

When he returned home that evening he told Margot that they needed to do something. Margot looked at him in surprise.

"What would we do?" She asked.

After a moment's silence, Robert replied.

"We're going to pay a visit to your family, we'll see how they are, and make sure that Lucy and your mother are doing well. Isn't that what you want?" He asked.

"Yes, but what if father is around?" She said nervously.

"Well, if he is, he is. But let's not let that stop you from seeing your family. If he tries anything, he'll have me to deal with. Don't you worry about that." He told her.

Margot looked at him with joy, she couldn't believe she's really going to see her family again. It felt so long since she'd had a chat with her sister. She'd missed it so much. She was overjoyed.

"When will we go?" She asked excitedly.

"No time like the present." Robert replied delighted at her happiness.

Margot slipped on the children's coats and shoes, before grabbing her shawl. Robert watched her tenderly, feeling a sense of warmth at what such a small gesture meant to her.

He watched as the two children grabbed Margot's hands and he gestured for them to pass through the door. As he followed them out he smiled gently at the sight of the three of them holding hands.

They took the short walk to where Margot's family lived. She couldn't help the deep feeling of relief to find that her father wasn't home. Robert watched as Margot took control of the situation. He even saw that once Margot was there that even her mother deferred to her. Lucy seems to be the only one not in awe of her sister, although she was obviously delighted to see her older sister.

Everybody gathered around Margot, wanting to know what she'd been doing these past months. Robert could see that they were a close knit family and loved each other dearly. He noticed that everyone seemed to be drawn to Margot. *She seems to be the glue holding this family together. They must have really missed her, now she doesn't live here any more,* he thought as he felt a warm feeling envelope his body.

He shook his head, as if to rid his head of these thoughts. *I can't be in love with this girl, she's been through so much she deserved something much better than me and my ready made family,* he thought. *No, I need to suppress these feelings until they disappear. Anyway, it's too soon after Mary for him to even contemplate another woman.*

He stood quietly in the corner smiling softly as he listened to the family chattering. They seem to have so much to catch up on and he feels gratified that he decided to bring her here. Once the hubbub had died down slightly, Margot introduced her family to Robert's children.

"This is Anna. She's five years old and a very clever young lady and this is Alfie, he's a bit over a year old and he's growing up to be a very handsome boy." She said smiling proudly at her two wards.

Margot's youngest brother laughed.

"I'm not the youngest any more." He said gleefully.

Everyone looked at him and laughed.

"You're right there Sam." Margot replied, patting him softly on the head.

As they were making merry, Walter arrived.

"What's going on?" He shouted above the noise

As he noticed Margot stood in the middle of the children his face went red with rage.

"What are you doing here? I told you never to come back. You'd better not 'ave done nothing to muddy the waters with that fishmonger. I might need another debt paid one of these days. Now get out and get back to where you belong." He shouted at her, spittle flying across the room.

The whole room froze as they came to the realisation that Walter had returned. Mabel turned from the crowd and went to prepare his supper and there wasn't a murmur from any of the children. Even Anna and Alfie seemed to know that they weren't to make a sound. Robert was shocked to see such a change in atmosphere as this awful man arrived home.

Walter started to stride towards the gathering. Margot cowered slightly as she was expecting a slap, or worse a punch. Before her father could get very far, he found a strong hand grabbing his shoulder. He hadn't realised that Robert was stood just inside of the door.

Robert moved to stand in front of Walter, and put his large hand around his throat, pushing him against the wall.

"Don't you ever touch Margot or any of her family again. Do you hear me?"

Walter gulped and nodded.

"Furthermore Margot will visit whenever she likes, and if she does want to leave us, then that is up to her, not you, not me because there's no way that you are going to get any more money out of me. You've had enough already. Is that clear?" He said furiously.

Being the bully that he was, Walter wasn't about to stand up to Robert. He nodded meekly, his eyes open as big as saucers. He looked distraught, and defeated. Robert let him go and Walter put his hand to his throat before moving as fast as he dared towards the table, where he slumped down into a chair, with his head in his hands.

The rest of the family stood there in shock. They'd never seen anyone get the better of their father before and didn't know quite what to do. Robert and Margot stayed a little longer, but the atmosphere was a little subdued and uncomfortable, now that Walter was in their midst.

Margot noticed Annie and Alfie yawning and smiled at her family.

"It's time to go, but I'll see you again really soon." She said quietly, not wanting to give Walter an opportunity to make a nasty comment. Not that it seemed, he'd slunk into his chair and didn't appear to be listening to the horde around him.

They all crowded round her to hug her, before Lucy pulled them away to allow Margot to pick up her shawl to leave.

CHAPTER FIFTEEN

After Margot had said her goodbyes, they started on their return journey home. As Margot walked beside Robert, she took a few tentative glances at her host. Looking at him with fresh eyes, she saw a man who seemed different somehow, less abrupt and much more kind and caring.

Eventually he noticed her looking at him.

"Is everything okay?" he asked?

"Yes." Smiled Margot.

"Did I go too far, back there, when I had a go at your father?" He asked pointing to the way they'd come from.

"Oh, no. Not at all." She replied.

Margot paused for a moment, not sure exactly how to word the deep gratitude she was feeling towards the man stood by her side.

"I'd like to thank you for what you just done. It were so kind of you. Thank you ever so much for being such a good person." She said eventually.

Robert held her gaze a little longer than he felt comfortable with, and nodded, before turning back to the road and continue to walk as if the conversation hadn't just taken place. He hadn't known how to respond to her words and felt a little embarrassed about the feelings he was starting to develop for her.

She's had such a hard life. She's a strong young woman who is kind and generous to Anna and Alfie, which I like very much. In fact, I like quite a few things about her, he thought as they continued walking.

What he didn't realise was that Margot was having similar thoughts. *He's been so cold and distant towards me, I didn't think he liked me very much and knowing the reason I was looking after his children, I'm not surprised. But I've seen another side of him today, one that I quite like. I know he's kind to the children, even if he doesn't show his emotions very often. But what he did for me today was totally unexpected,* she thought, as she tried to keep up with him.

They both continued the journey in silence, not knowing what else to say to each other. They seemed to have found out a lot about each other over these past few hours, and were trying to process exactly what that meant for their relationship. As they walked, Alfie started to get grumpy.

"I'm tired." He complained.

The adults looked at each other and laughed, which broke the ice somewhat.

"'Ere, let me carry you." Robert told him.

Alfie held up his arms to be picked up.

"What about you Anna?" Margot asked.

"Im a bit tired, but I'm okay, thanks Margot." Anna replied smiling up at her.

As soon as they got inside, Robert took Alfie to the bed and pulled the blanket over him. Margot helped Anna get her nightdress on and tucked her in, with a gentle kiss on her forehead.

"I'm tired too." Said Margot. "It's been quite an eventful evening."

"Good night" replied Robert smiling at her.

Margot turned to the bed which was partly hidden by a modesty sheet, where she changed into her bedclothes before turning in.

"Thank you again." She said smiling as she settled down to sleep.

Robert stayed up a little while longer, pondering on what had occurred that evening.

The next day Margot was just leaving to do her grocery shopping, when she bumped into Mrs Baker, who lived next door.

"Good morning my dear." Mrs Baker said.

"Good morning Mrs Baker." Margot replied.

"You was out a bit late last night?" Mrs Baker said in a questioning tone.

Margot smiled, *you can't do nothing round 'ere without someone noticing*, she thought. Not that she minded. She'd grown up in these parts and quite liked the fact that your neighbours would look out for you. Help you out if they could

"Yes," she replied. Mr Clark was helping me with a problem." She explained, hoping Mrs Baker wouldn't want too much detail.

"He's a good man, though much quieter now that his

wife died." Mrs Baker replied.

Margot nodded, hoping that Mrs Baker would tell her more about Robert. Now she'd seen another side of him, she was quite curious to know more.

"Yes, dear, Hope you don't mind me saying, but 'e seems to have gone back into his shell, now that she's not about. He was a bit like that when he first arrived, but she soon had him laughing and joking around. They even invited us around for drinks a few times. But since she died I've not stepped foot in that house.

"Oh." Exclaimed Margot. "I didn't realise. He always seems very quiet, very reserved to me. But there's another side to him then?"

"Yes, I think he just needs a good woman to bring him out his shell." Mrs Baker said winking at Margot.

Margot blushed, saying, "Well, I'd better get off."

Mrs Baker smiled as she recognised the first signs of a new romance.

As Margot went about her chores she started thinking over what Mrs Baker had told her.

Feeling more kindly towards Robert, she wondered why he had changed so much. *Maybe he tried to block his feelings out when she died,* she thought. *he may not have wanted to put him or the children in that position again. I should of been more understanding. I mean, it's not been very long really since she died. I suppose it takes a long time to get over something like that.*

The house was gleaming by the time Robert returned. He came in and took off his coat and sat down.

"Good day?" Margot asked brightly

Robert looked at her surprised. *She never asks about my day?* He thought.

"It was busy, and cold today. I'm glad I got that thick coat." He replied politely.

Margot smiled warmly at him and went to sort out the evening meal.

Robert watched as she pottered around getting things ship shape and Bristol fashioned. *She seems to have softened towards me. I wonder if there's any chance she may feel the same way that I'm starting to feel about her?* He thought.

He shook his head. *No, it can't be that, she's young and attractive, she won't want to be stuck with a ready made family. She's just grateful, that's all, for what I did so she can see her family. I better not tell her how I feel,*

I'll just going to let sleeping dogs lie.

CHAPTER SIXTEEN

Over the next couple of weeks, things settled into a nice routine. Robert was more kindly towards Margot and they would sit down of an evening and chat about their respective days. The children noticed that they were getting on well and Anna especially become more lively and relaxed around her father. Margot was delighted to see how Anna was gaining in confidence and did everything she could to encourage her.

Even though she'd been desperate to leave at one time, now she this was the last thing she wanted. She loved the children with all her heart and had come to the realisation that she had feelings for Robert. She wasn't yet sure what those feelings were, but each day they seemed to get that little bit closer and she had come to care about him. However, she was too shy to say anything because she didn't think that he would feel the same about her. *No, Robert is probably still grieving his wife. It's best to say nothing and enjoy his company for what it is*, she decided.

One evening as she was returning from a visit to see her family, she pushed open the door slightly to hear Anna and Robert talking.

"Is Margot going to be our new mother?"

Margot decided to stay outside as she was interested to hear how Robert responded.

She heard from the deep intake of breath that he was surprised at the question.

Of course, I doubt He's even thought of me in that way, she thought disappointedly.

She held her breath for his response

"No, of course not." Robert said reflexively, not wanting his daughter to get her hopes up.

Margot chewed her lip as she watched Anna's head go down and tears start to well up in her eyes. She was desperate to run to Anna and comfort her, but she also wanted to hear what else Robert had to say.

Robert put his arms around his daughter.

"Me and Margot, we're just friends. One day she'll want to move on with her life and we'll have to let her."

Margot had heard enough and pushed the door open quickly. Robert stood there looking guilty, hoping that Margot hadn't heard their conversation. *I don't want her getting the wrong end of the stick,* he thought. *She might feel obligated to stay if she thinks she's needed.*

He quickly changed topic.

"I'm just going to put Anna to bed." He said.

Feeling hurt and upset, Margot didn't know how to react to what she'd just heard. She loved the children, but *if Robert doesn't feel the same way about me as I do about him, then maybe I shouldn't stay where I'm not wanted*, she thought angrily.

Noticing Margot frowning he said, "Unless you want to do it?"

"No, it's fine. You can do it. She's your daughter after all." Margot said abruptly.

Robert looked surprised at her tone and wondered why she was so upset. He thought back to see if he could remember upsetting her in any way.

No, he decided. She was fine when she left. *Maybe*

something happened with her father tonight, that put her out of sorts? Should I ask her? No, I'm sure she don't want me interfering. I expect everything will be back to normal in the morning.

Margot went to bed early that night. She had a decision to make and she didn't want her feelings for Robert hampering her thoughts. She pretended to fall asleep quickly, but in fact tossed and turned until the early hours of the morning trying to make sure she made the right choice.

Eventually she decided that she had to leave. There was no way she could stay there knowing that he would never love her, as she loved him. So before anybody could awake, she got up and quietly got dressed. She grabbed as much of her stuff as she could manage and tiptoed towards the door. As she went to pull the door shut, she looked over at them lying in their beds. She was going to miss them so much.

CHAPTER SEVENTEEN

The next morning, Robert woke to find the room was cold. He got up and noticed that the fire hadn't been lit and breakfast wasn't on the table. He looked around, but could see no sign of Margot, which surprised him. Not once had she not had breakfast waiting for the rest of them when they awoke, not since the first day when Robert had told her what her duties were.

He strode over to the bed, but Margot wasn't there. He gently shook his daughter awake.

"Anna, where's Margot? Has she gone out?" He whispered, not wanting to disturb Alfie.

Anna slowly opened her eyes and blearily looked around.

"Uh?" she said, still not fully awake.

"Have you seen Margot?" Robert asked a little more sharply.

Anna sat up in bed and looked around bewildered.

"Has Margot gone out?" she asked.

"That's what I'm trying to find out." He replied. "What would she likely be wearing if she'd gone out early?" He asked.

"I don't know." Replied Anna. "She didn't say nothing to me."

Robert left Anna to wake up fully and looked around once more, *like she could hide in here!* He thought shaking his head at his foolishness. He opened the front door and looked up and down the street to see if she was there. But he couldn't see anything. She had definitely gone somewhere. He just didn't know where.

He made some bread and jam for the three of them to eat, *I managed before Margot, though I'm not sure I want to find out if I can still manage,* he thought. He was desperate to go searching for Margot, but didn't want the children to know how worried he was.

"Aren't you going to work today?" Anna asked.

Robert shook his head.

"I thought I would have a day off. Maybe walk you to school." He said.

Anna smiled at the idea of walking to school with her dad. He was normally too busy.

He hurried back from school in the hope that Margot would be waiting for them on his return. He quickly pushed open the door and went inside. He looked around and saw that it was empty.

"Margot?" Alfie whimpered.

"It's okay little boy, I'm going to find her." He said hopefully.

After a couple of hours, he decided he couldn't wait any longer. *What if something has happened to her*, he thought. *What if her dad got at her while I wasn't around to protect her and he did something to her. I know I should have pushed it last night. I'll never forgive myself if he's hit her again*. He grabbed his coat and scooping Alfie up in his arms he went next door to ask Mrs Baker's if she would keep an eye on Alfie.

"What was Margot doing early this morning, carrying her belongings?" Mrs Baker asked as she took Alfie in her arms.

"You what?" Said Robert gruffly.

"I seen her scurrying past, early doors, I know. I never sleep well and I was just getting some water when she passed by."

"Oh, she's definitely gone then," said Robert quietly under his breath, disconcerted by the news.

"Lover's tiff, was it?" Mrs Baker asked.

"Don't be silly. There's nothing going on between me and Margot." Robert told her.

"Not yet, but I see the way you two look at each other. You better not let 'er go. She's a good'un." Mrs Baker warned him.

Robert left, confused. Mrs Barker must be mistaken. There was no way that Margot could love him. He decided that his first port of call would be her family. Maybe her mother or Lucy had seen her or at least knew if there was something bothering her.

He knocked frantically on the door, and her mother answered it.

"Hello, Robert. How nice to see you. What can I do for you?"

"Can I come in a minute?" He asked. "It's about Margot."

Mabel opened the door and stood back to allow

Robert to enter, then she closed the door behind her and leaned against it.

"What's the matter?" She asked anxiously. "Is she in trouble?"

"She's disappeared. Apparently she left in the middle of the night. I don't know where she's gone. I was hoping that she'd come here." Robert explained frantically.

"I've not seen her, what makes you think she's left?" Mabel asked.

Robert told her that their neighbour had seen her scurrying down the street, with a bag of her belongings.

"I hoped she'd be here. I didn't know where else to look." He said

"Maybe at the factory?" Mabel suggested. "But I doubt it really. Why would she have gone anyway?" She asked

"Did anything happen yesterday when she visited?"

"No." Mabel replied, frowning and trying to think back to anything that might have happened. "Why?"

"Well when she got back she was in a bad mood and then when I woke up this morning, she wasn't there. That's why I was hoping that she'd be here with you."

Mabel shook her head.

"I've not seen her. Not since last night, and I'm sure she was okay when she left."

Robert, looked her and thought, *what happened to put her in a bad mood then?*

Thinking back to when she'd arrived home, he sunk down into the nearest chair.

"She must have overheard the conversation I was having with Anna." He said, as he seemed to deflate in front of Mabel.

"What was it about?" She asked.

"But why would it have upset her. I was just trying to make Anna understand that just because we love Margot, it doesn't mean that she loved us. Well, unless what Mrs Baker was saying was true?"

Mabel looked at him with a curious expression on her face.

He looked up at Mabel.

"If you see her, will you tell her I love her. I said those things to Anna to protect her, I didn't think for one moment that she might love me, but if she does, please tell her to come home."

Mabel smiled and nodded.

She looked behind Robert and he followed her gaze. Margot was standing there, tears of joy falling down her cheeks.

"You really love me?" She asked Robert.

He nodded unable to speak.

Mabel looked on delighted as Margot ran to Robert and put her arms around him. Robert looked down at her with a huge smile on his face. He kissed her on the top of her head.

"Will you be my wife?" He asked as he took her face in his hands.

"Yes, of course." Margot shouted out gleefully.

"I think we might have some explaining to do to Anna." Robert said smiling. "I think she might be delighted in having you for her new mother."

"Not as happy as I'm going to be." Margot promised him.

As they were chatting excitedly, Walter made an appearance.

"What's going on?" He asked

"They're getting married. Isn't it exciting." Mabel

said, forgetting for once how scared she was of her husband.

Walter rubbed his hands in glee. He knew the fishmonger had a bit of cash, and if he played his cards right, maybe he could cash in on the marriage.

"What wonderful news." He said. "And to think, it was me that introduced you to each other.

Margo and Robert looked over at each other and smiled, deciding that this wasn't the time to start an argument.

CHAPTER EIGHTEEN

Margot woke with butterflies in her stomach. Trying to swallow her nervousness she sat up and looked around. This was a house she'd grown up in and she'd woken up with her sister snuggled into her. Margot had forgotten how crowded the bed could get, when she shared it with the rest of her sisters. She recalled how when she'd been living there, how they'd all scratch about before going to sleep trying to grab a little piece of the blanket, hoping they wouldn't wake up cold during the night.

She gently disengaged herself and walked the few steps it took to get to the stove. She sat down with her chin in her hands and started thinking about the past few months. Since Robert had made his feelings known, life had been wonderful. She still slept with the children, and was actually a little nervous about moving to sleep with Robert, once she was married later today.

She was glad that she'd decided to stay over. Lucy was going to help her get ready, but first they needed to have breakfast. Margot put the fire on, and filled the kettle with water. By the time the kettle was boiling her mother and Lucy had joined her.

"It's your wedding day." Lucy reminded her excitedly.

"I know." Laughed Margot. "I've been up ages, getting everything ready."

After breakfast Lucy took charge.

"Go get your dress." She demanded.

Margot nodded and scampered over to the chair where she'd carefully laid it out so it wouldn't get creased. Miraculously none of the younger children had touched it and it remained clean. Lucy sat Margot down and pulled her hair up into a bun, using pins to add in small wild flowers here and there.

She took the small cracked mirror that the family shared and put it in front of Margot.

"Oh Lucy, I look beautiful." Margot said, tears welling up behind her eyes.

"You always look beautiful." Replied Lucy smiling at her beloved sister.

Margot held out her arms to Lucy who stepped into her warm embrace and they took a minute to be grateful of their strength and fortitude.

"I'm going to miss you." Lucy said.

"I left ages ago." Margot said giggling.

"But it won't be the same. You'll be having children of your own. You'll be too busy to visit."

"Then you'll have to visit me." Replied Margot. "I might need help with baby-sitting."

While Lucy got herself dressed, Margot took a minute to think over the past twelve months.

"I hope I make a good wife." She said as Lucy came over to show her what she looked like.

"Of course you will. Why do you think you might not. You're so good with Anna and Alfie. They love you like their your own."

"I know. But you know…" Margot paused. "Tonight, what if I make a mistake?"

Lucy looked at her sister who was usually so confident and laughed gently at her.

"I'm sure it'll be fine. After all Robert knows what he's doing." She chided.

"I suppose so." Said Margot, giggling nervously.

"I can't believe I'm a bridesmaid. I'm so happy." Lucy said, changing the subject. It wasn't something she had any experience with, so didn't feel comfortable giving any advice.

Margot looked at her gratefully. She had enough to worry about with the wedding, she'd worry about the wedding night later. She grabbed the brush and sat her sister down, helping her pull back her hair into a neat bun.

It was a short walk to the church, so once everyone was ready, they made a fine procession down to the churchyard. Lucy clutched Margot's arm, whispering excitedly to her.

"Anyone would think this was your wedding not mine." Laughed Margot.

"I'm just so happy for you." Lucy said smiling widely.

"I know you are and I love you for it." Margot said in a more serious tone.

"And I love you, dear sister." Replied Lucy.

Robert was already standing at the altar and he

watched in delight as Margot walked slowly down the aisle. She looked over at her family watching her and then glanced at where Anna and Alfie were sat. *My new family. I'm so grateful that they love me as much as I love them. Anna took the news so well, that I was to be married to her father*, she thought as she tried to blank out her nerves.

After the wedding, Walter sidled up to Robert.

"Fancy a drink to celebrate?" He asked

Robert shook his head. He didn't mind having a cup or two occasionally, but he wasn't really a drinker, plus he knew Walter just wanted to cadge off him.

"Thanks, but no." he replied. "Anyway, haven't the girls put on a spread back at the house?"

"Please yourself." Said Walter, shrugging before turning in the direction of the alehouse.

The rest of them traipsed back to the house where, with Walter's absence helping them all to relax, they had a big celebration, with food and dancing, as best as they could in their small abode.

As Margo was talking to her mother, she felt a tug on her on a dress. She looked around, and it was both Anna, and Alfie.

"Hello, my darlings. What can I do for you?"

"We just want to tell you how happy we are, that we've got you as a mother." Anna said smiling adoringly at Margot.

"Thank you Anna. I love you very much. That means so much to me, and your birth mother will alway be here in spirit." Margot said smiling.

Finally the celebrations came to an end. Robert carried Anna and Margot took Alfie in her arms. They trudged back happily and dropped the two children into their bed.

"It won't hurt them just one night to sleep in their day clothes." Robert whispered.

"I agree." Smiled Margot, nervous as to what was going to happen next.

Robert took her by the hand and led her to his bed, where they quietly made love until the sun was just about to come up. Finally they lay in each other's arms and fell into a deep and relaxed sleep.

And when Margot woke the next day, she thought back to the night before and laughed at herself for ever being worried about it.

THE KITCHEN MAID'S SALVATION

CHAPTER ONE

Mabel lay down on the bed, unable to keep her pale grey eyes open any longer. Her dark blonde hair splayed out underneath her, as she let out a big sigh. She loved her job, but she was always glad when the day came to an end.

She had been a kitchen maid for the Wethertons since she was fifteen years old, helping Cook prepare the meals for the family.

Her aunt had known Catherine Ainsworth since she was a child and the housekeeper had asked if she knew of a child with good character to fill the position of scullery maid. She'd quickly mentioned her niece to Catherine and so Mabel had found herself in service at just ten years old.

She'd been scared at first, leaving her family home, but had quickly adapted to the servants life. She was well fed, with a clean bed and had access to private washing facilities, which was more than she would have got at home.

Mabel was hard-working and went about her work with a smile on her face. She was always polite and respectful of her superiors and so when the kitchen maid left to get married the cook had asked if she'd be willing to take over the duties.

Mabel had jumped at the chance and with the housekeeper's blessing had been working as the kitchen maid for the past two years.

She had been devastated when her parents and two younger brothers had become unwell with tuberculosis. She had wanted to go and visit them, but Mrs Ainsworth had forbid her to do so. Although Cook has been quite indignant about Catherine giving such orders she secretly agreed with her. *I don't like the thought of her bringing back any diseases,* she told herself, even though she had felt sorry for the girl.

She had cried for days when they died one by one. The only thing she was grateful for was that her mother had been the last to die, so she'd been there for her brothers when they passed.

Edna had thought they were going to have to call the

doctor in as Mabel had been hysterical. A couple of days later, she pulled herself together and acted like it had never happened. The cook wasn't sure if this was helpful, but Mabel seemed happy enough so she let her be.

Mabel often thought about her family and was determined to make something of herself, so they would be proud of her. The only family she had left was her aunt Charlotte. Mabel didn't know her well and her only recent memory was when she'd visited just after the funeral, which Mabel hadn't been allowed to go to.

Aunt Charlotte had been quite stern and had told her not to do anything to bring disrepute to their family honour. Mabel had been terrified of this tall woman, dressed all in black that looked at her as though she was too much to bear.

Mabel shook her head, *Enough of that, I've got work to do,* she told herself as she realised Edna was talking to her.

She nodded. "Yes Mrs Peabody. I'll do it straight away." She said, turning to the pantry to look for the ingredients to make scones for afternoon tea.

Edna smiled at the young girl. *She's a good girl,* she thought as she turned back to the oven to take out the pie that she had made for lunch. She knew that Mabel liked her job and so she took great enjoyment at teaching her new dishes. *After all she might have my job one day,* thought Edna.

Mabel loved her job and though she didn't think of herself as being ambitious, she would have been over the moon to know that Edna thought that she might be capable of one day taken over her role.

The Wethercote's house was situated on the edge of town. It was of gothic design, with stone mullioned windows and a detailed facade. It was surrounded by a large garden, with stone steps up to the front door, and a servant's entrance around the back of the house.

The Wethercote's had two daughters, but Mabel had never spoken to them. They had been too young when she'd been working upstairs and now her job as kitchen maid didn't often take her our of the kitchen. The only people she had any real dealings with were Cook and Emma, the scullery maid who had taken over from Mabel when she herself had moved to the kitchen.

She would see Mrs Ainsworth and Mr Harris, the butler during meal times, but they both looked down their noses at having to speak with the likes of her, so she did her best not to make eye contact with them.

She shared a room with Emma but she didn't really class her as a friend. By the end of the day, they were both exhausted from their duties and so their only proper conversations were during their short meal breaks.

Mabel loved looking out of the deep sash windows onto the south-facing garden, where she could look at the flower beds planted to the side and the beautiful wisteria which climbed the rear of the property.

It's not a bad life here I suppose, she thought, as she spent a minute looking out at the roses which were starting to show new growth.

OTHER BOOKS BY THIS AUTHOR

Queenie's Endeavours

Queenie is the only child of an Irish couple who came to England to search for a better life.She's given the opportunity to be a maid for a wealthy family and after bumping into a handsome young man, she thinks that life is looking rosy.

Joseph has just been accepted for police training and cannot wait to start his new career. Bumping into a pretty girl on the way home is the icing on the cake.

Events transpire that pull Queenie out of her comforting environment and threaten everything she's ever wanted.

Every endeavour she makes to sort out her life seems to take her further away from where she wants to be.

Will Queenie be forced into a life she doesn't want to protect her nearest and dearest, or can she find a way back to those she loves

The Kitchen Maid's Salvation

A heartwarming victorian historical fiction romance

Mabel is an orphaned kitchen maid who finds herself through no fault of her own with child.

After being thrown out on the streets she finds herself alone and lost. A kind stranger takes her in, but everything isn't as she thought and she's lucky to escape.

Joseph is a policeman who meets Mabel after she comes into the station to make a complaint.

Will her past prevent them from building a future together or will Joseph give her a second chance for happiness?

Printed in Great Britain
by Amazon

21776439R00066